Pete Puffin's
WiLD RiDE

Cruising Alaska's Currents

Written and Illustrated
by Libby Hatton

Alaska Geographic Association
Anchorage, Alaska

Ahoy there!

I'm Pete Puffin and this is the story of my far-out Alaska adventure, riding rivers in the sea.

Long ago, Eddy Turn's grandfather carved me from the hardest oak and painted me with the brightest marine paints. I look like the birds he saw in Alaska when he was young.

Eddy took me everywhere.

Most summers, the Turns drove to their cabin on the Maine coast.

But one summer...

3

PUFFIN EXPLORER

...Eddy stuffed my furry friend, Ted, and me into a backpack.
Eddy's family was going on a cruise to Alaska.

I was so excited. Alaska is home to horned
puffins just like me.

With a deep blast of the horn, our ship steamed
out of the harbor and headed north.

SHIP
BOARDING
FOR
ALASKA

ALASKA

N. PACIFIC CURRENT

INSIDE PASSAGE

ALASKA MARINE
HIGHWAY

LANDLUBBERS

4

Every day, Eddy took Ted and me for a stroll around the ship's deck. Ted was hanging limp from all the ocean motion and in danger of losing his stuffing. As for me, Pete Puffin, I'm a sea bird, born to rock and roll on the ocean waves.

Our ship steered through the islands of Southeast Alaska.

We saw salmon caught in big seine nets.

We shivered at tongues of ice flowing out of mountain valleys to the sea.

We gaped at fishing boats hauling huge flat-faced halibut from the sea floor.

Soon the ship glided into fog so thick that I could hardly see the end of my own bright beak. When the fog lifted, no land was in sight. We were cruising in the open ocean.

The ship's loud speaker boomed, **"Whale off the starboard bow!"**

Everyone rushed to watch the whale. Eddy held Ted and me over the railing so we could see.

Then I felt Eddy's hand slip...

"Bird overboard!"

I heard Eddy crying, but his calls for help grew fainter and fainter...

The cruise ship disappeared beyond the edge of my watery world.
I floated alone; a small wooden bird in an endless sea.

11

I was so scared I could hardly think.

Back then, I knew nothing about our blue planet Earth. Blue because it is covered with oceans which move in currents.

Like rivers in the sea, these currents flow warm or cold, sweep up or down, swing east or west or north or south. Currents control the ocean and the weather—and right then, they were controlling me.

Like a giant washing machine, the great North Pacific currents carried me as they swirled and curled all the way from Alaska out toward Japan and back again.

As the earth turns it creates wind and ocean currents

ARCTIC OCEAN

BEAUFORT SEA

CHUKCHI SEA

RUSSIA

ALASKA

CANADA

PUFFIN EXPLORER
OCEAN CURRENTS
MY ADVENTURE
WHERE I FELL X

BERING SEA

ALEUTIAN ISLANDS

ALASKAN STREAM

ALASKA CURRENT

PACIFIC OCEAN

You can follow my journey on this map that shows some really cool currents.

All I wanted was to be back home with Eddy. But around I went for more than a year, 'round and 'round like the current that trapped me.

Sometimes I'd think, *I'm Pete Puffin, a sea bird. My natural home is water*, and I would feel brave. Then I'd think, *Oh, I'm just a little wooden toy. I miss Eddy and Ted!* and I'd feel very down.

Fall came, and then winter.
The ocean was wild.

In the spring, I discovered I wasn't alone after all. Tiny plants bloomed in the sea, and more ocean creatures arrived to eat them.

The little plants were gobbled up by lots of little animals, which were then slurped up by the bigger animals.

Everyone depended on the hearty "soup" of these small plants and animals served up by the currents. Even whales as big as buses strained them through their comb-like baleen.

Sometimes I was in danger of being on the menu...

THE INVISIBLE GARDEN UNDER THE MICROSCOPE

TEENY TINY PLANTS

LITTLE BITTY ANIMALS

...or of drowning under tangles of junk left behind in the ocean.

SHIPPING CONTAINERS FALL OFF

80,000 NIKE SHOES SPILLED

28,800 BATH TOYS LOST OVERBOARD

34,000 HOCKEY GLOVES MISSING AT SEA

REWARD OFFERED

6,000,000 PLASTIC BAGS FOUND IN NORTH PACIFIC OCEAN

MADE IN

KEEP OCEANS CLEAN

I saw big ships and fishing fleets. My hopes rose.

Now I'll be rescued.

But the folks on the boats never seemed to see me. I guess I looked like one more puffin on a fishing trip.

Lots of other seabirds kept me company. I loved watching the puffins dive for fish.

During one summer of my adventure, I was whipping past Alaska's Aleutian Islands again when a monster storm blew me right between some islands...

...and into the Bering Sea.

Here hungry animals feasted on
the Bering Sea buffet. Walrus
gulped down clams, sea lions
chomped on bottom fish and
cormorants and their cousins
swallowed capelin whole.
Some orcas feasted on salmon, while
others hunted sea lions. All busily eating,
just like passengers on cruise ships.

I saw boats out there too. Some were
pulling up big cages called crab pots.

Suddenly I was riding on top of a cage full of cranky crabs.

I am rescued at last! I'll see Eddy again soon!

But I fell off and disappeared under a wave.

I drifted in despair.

Eventually, currents swept me into the Arctic Ocean, on the far northern side of Alaska.

I was trapped in the groaning, bumping, squealing ice pack. Just when I thought I'd be splintered into a thousand toothpicks, a curious seal flipped me onto the ice.

DANGER!
THIN ICE

I rode across the top of the world for several long winters, watching ribbons of northern lights dance among the stars.

But even there I wasn't alone.

Lucky for me, I didn't taste like seal. The white giant bit my tail, dumped me into the drink and ambled off to find a better breakfast.

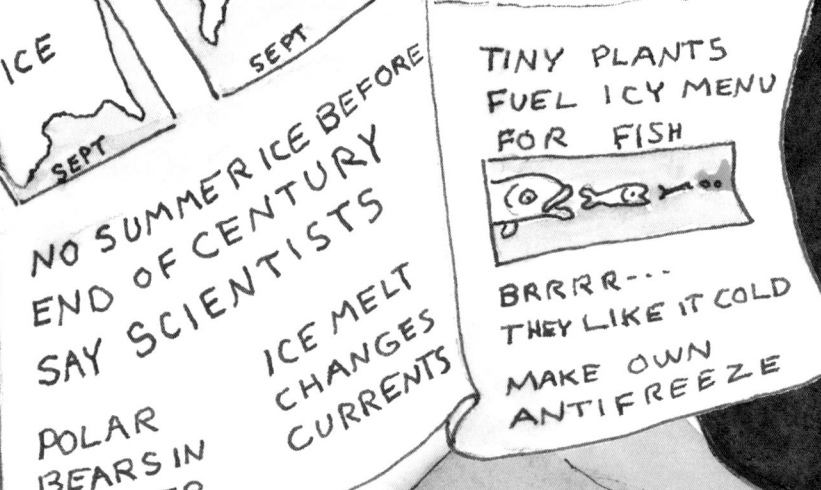

NEWS

ARCTIC ICE MELTS

25 YEARS AGO

ICE

SEPT

NOW

ICE

SEPT

NO SUMMER ICE BEFORE
END OF CENTURY
SAY SCIENTISTS

POLAR
BEARS IN
DANGER

ICE MELT
CHANGES
CURRENTS

LOTS OF LIFE
FOUND IN SEA
ICE

TINY PLANTS
FUEL ICY MENU
FOR FISH

BRRRR···
THEY LIKE IT COLD
MAKE OWN
ANTIFREEZE

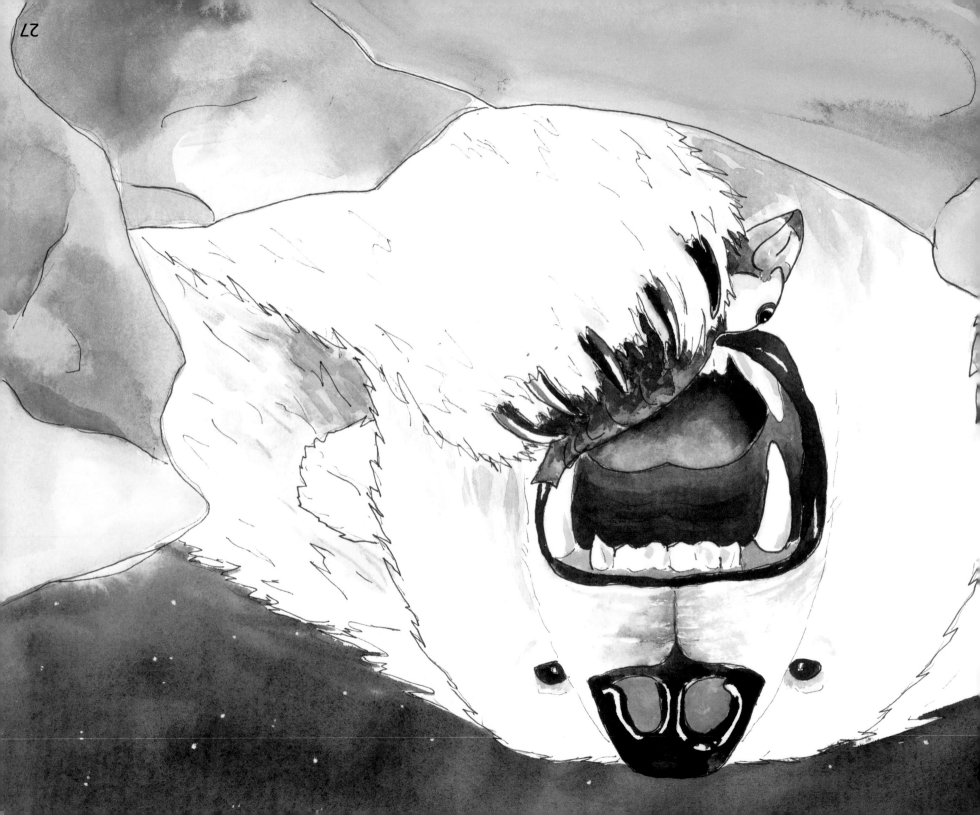

Late one summer, I was heading south into the Atlantic Ocean, barely afloat.

The sea rose, whipped into a frenzy from a hurricane. Waves whirled and whacked me and buried me under tons of water, then coughed me back up. A wall of waves hurled me past a lighthouse toward a strangely familiar shore. A mountainous wave flung me onto a rocky beach.

Seaweed saved me. Bruised but not broken, I
dreamed away a winter on those weedy rocks.

When summer came, I heard kids laughing and shouting on the beach.

Suddenly a little girl held me high.

Her big brother laughed. Then he peered closely at me.

He was my Eddy, now a grown boy.

"Mom, Dad, Gramps, look what Katie found!"

Home at last with my very own family.

Eddy scrubbed away the seaweed and barnacles, and Katie tucked me in beside old Ted. He was missing an eye and seemed a bit crotchety.

Every night I tell Ted all about my wild ride, cruising Alaska's currents.

31

Hey kids, Pete Puffin's wild ride may seem like a fairy tale. Believe-it-or-not, it's based on a true story.

Back in 1992, a cargo ship heading from Asia to America got caught in a terrible storm. Pitching and rolling on the sea like a feather in the wind, the massive ship lost twelve containers overboard. One of those held 28,800 yellow duckies, blue turtles, green frogs, and red beavers. The plastic toys, which normally float only in the calm waters of bathtubs, were tossed into the wide open sea.

Currents picked up the toys and carried them along. Around and around the North Pacific Ocean they went. Toys landed on beaches in far-flung places like Russia, Hawaii, Alaska, Canada, and Washington to be found by beachcombers. Some were pushed north through to the Arctic Ocean and around the North Pole to the Atlantic. Twelve years after the spill in 2003, one of the toys was found on the coast of Maine. Another was found in Scotland. And the toys continue to be found.

Duckies aren't the only thing floating in the ocean's currents. Every year about 10,000 containers spill from cargo ships sending flotsam out to ride the rivers in the sea. This drifting debris is studied by oceanographers who use knowledge about ocean currents to predict and track the fate of flotsam.

MY PUFFIN FAMILY

BIG GUY — TUFTED

HANDSOME ONE — HORNED

EASTERNER — ATLANTIC

COUSIN — RHINOCEROS AUKLET

PUFFIN LIFE

STORMS · FLYING TO LAND · BREEDING COLORS · NESTING · EGG · BABY · PREDATOR ANIMALS · PREDATOR FISH · FLYING OUT TO SEA · PREDATOR BIRDS · FISHING · DIVING FOR FISH · FISH NETS

ALGAE + BACTERIA · BABY FISH · TINY ANIMALS LIKE SHRIMP

IF THE OCEAN WARMS TOO MUCH, THE FISH THAT LIKE COLD WATER WILL DISAPPEAR.

PUFFINS WILL HAVE FEWER FISH TO BRING TO THEIR BABIES AND THE BABIES WILL STARVE.